2 476619 21
D0243992

DADDY FARTYPANTS

EMER STAMP • MATT HUNT

For Dick Stamp, the original
Daddy Fartypants – E.S.

For my family – M.H.

ORCHARD BOOKS

First published in Great Britain in 2019 by
The Watts Publishing Group

1 3 5 7 9 10 8 6 4 2

Text © Emer Stamp 2019
Illustrations © Matt Hunt 2019

The moral rights of the author and
illustrator have been asserted.

All rights reserved.

A CIP catalogue record for this book is
available from the British Library.

HB ISBN 978 1 40835 633 3
PB ISBN 978 1 40835 635 7

MIX
Paper from
responsible sources
FSC® C104740
FSC
www.fsc.org

Printed and bound in China

Orchard Books
An imprint of Hachette Children's Group
Part of The Watts Publishing Group Limited
Carmelite House, 50 Victoria Embankment
London EC4Y 0DZ

An Hachette UK Company
www.hachette.co.uk

www.hachettechildrens.co.uk

DADDY FARTYPANTS

RENFREWSHIRE COUNCIL	
247661921	
Bertrams	10/04/2019
	£6.99
BIS	

EMER STAMP • MATT HUNT

ORCHARD

Daddy Fartypants
was a very windy bear.

RRRRRIP!
"Dad!"

It didn't matter where he was . . .

RUMBLE
"Dad!"

. . . or what he was doing . . .

his bottom blasts were **epic**.
And to make matters worse . . .

Daddy Fartypants always, always,
ALWAYS blamed someone else.

PAAARRRP!
"The old bear!"
"Err?"
"The bear on the telly!"
BRRRUP!

Even when it was REALLY obvious, Daddy Fartypants never said "sorry" or "pardon", or "excuse me, please".

No, Daddy Fartypants never,
ever, ever, ever, EVER . . .

PWAAAA
. . . owned up.
SPROUTS
BEANS
"It was my boy!"

AAAAARD!
"Dad!!!!!"

POOP
"What did I do?"

"Humph!"

SCHOOL

Then, one day after school, Daddy Fartypants met the lovely new teacher, Miss Lovelybear.

But as he went to shake her hand . . .

Miss Lovelybear let out a rip-roaring . . .
BWWWWAAAR
"Yuck!"
"Disgusting!"
"Pooey!"
"What DID you have for lunch?"

Everyone heard it.

But Miss Lovelybear didn't say "sorry" or "pardon" or "excuse me, please". Instead she said . . .

"It wasn't me . . .

it was HIM!"

Daddy Fartypants was shocked.

"W . . . what?"

He was outraged.

"How dare you!"

He was upset.

"Everyone thinks it was ME!"

But, most of all, he was ashamed.

And that night he made a promise . . .

"I do beg your pardon. That was me."
SQUEEEEEAK!
"Ah, Dad."

Daddy Fartypants is STILL a very windy bear. But no matter where he is . . .

SILENCE
PLEASE
"SHHHHH!"

. . . or what he's doing . . .

. . . he always, always, always, **always** . . .

PPPP